I0526776

First Love

Poems for Ross

First Love

Poems for Ross

The hard part is not discovering love,
but destroying the barriers in you
you have built to keep it out.
—Rumi

—————

by AC Benus

—————

an AC Benus Impression
San Francisco

*Grateful acknowledgement is here offered
for the support and encouragement
I've received on the literary site*
www.gayauthors.org.

ISBN 978-1-7345610-8-1 (ebook)
ISBN 978-1-7345610-9-8 (paperback)

FIRST LOVE: POEMS FOR ROSS.
Copyright © 2020 by AC Benus.
All rights reserved.
No part of this book may be used or reproduced
in any manner whatsoever without written
permission, except in the case of brief quotations
embodied in critical articles and reviews.

Cover photo:
Mitch Braithwaite / unsplash.com

Double Heart & Hand vignette:
From an 18th century French volume of love poetry

Library of Congress Control Number: 2020910917

Ross was a sandy-haired, gray-eyed youth I fell in love with when I was nineteen and he was eighteen. We met at university, and he befriended me via a note passed in our math class, along with his beautiful, enigmatic smile. He was the first boy I ever loved.

As for the quality of the verse to follow, I'll paraphrase Messrs. Morris and Adams, who in an anthology of same-sex love poems, warn the readers the volume contains "a large number of pieces of less artistic excellence than usual, but which, nevertheless, are honest in sentiment and sure of appeal." Such lenient application of – or maybe, temporary suspension of – critical judgement should probably be considered appropriate when encountering expressions of a person's first love. What matters is connection from heart to heart before brain to brain.

ACB

Overview

Ode to those who understand
    that love's not grand

To those without peace of mind
    and hearts still to find

Beauty: painful, sullen still,
    still the eternal hill

To conquer love is to sing
    of the beauty of everything

Thus I've found you not to me
    simply because it's not to be

For what are earthly things too
    when I think of you?

Ode to those who understand
    that love's not grand.

Poem No. 1 [ii]

    I want to love you, I
want to embrace you, to
feel your warmth. I want
to caress your smile, and
feel your soft glowing hair.

    I want to take hold of your
shoulders and gently kiss the
back of your neck, moving to
seduce an ear.

    I want to caress and envelope
all the oensuality that I can give
upon you, until you, from
ecstasy can do nothing but
love and cherish me.

    I want to love you.

<u>Beauty, I want to sing of you</u>

Poem No. 2

Oblivious to you, the joy I do derive
from your simply being alive

So...

By torchlight and of candle still
I write of you and love in eloquence from my quill

Hair of moonbeams made to golden perfection
in the sun's ever soft direction

Eyes that sing not of earthly things
but, of radiant eternally-young life to bring

Cheeks softer than anyone ever need know
features of divine-like glow

Such light does live in your smile
Perfection's glow, I swear, all others this denied

Really, everything about your features does in me stir
thoughts of the ultimate lure

But more than your earthly traits discovered
your godly gifts give a chance for hope uncovered.

So…

By torchlight and of candle still
I write of you, and love, in eloquence from my quill.

Poem No. 3

Lyrics:

You are a radiant sun shining on an unworthy shore
    warming sweetly regions benign
    hidden though they are in the cold dark
You stimulate them with your light.

Your light draws love from a very deep place hidden
        from even me
    sweetly warming regions benign
    which I didn't realize were there
Your light, so gentle, do I need.

You are a radiant sun shining on an unworthy shore
    with your light can I take on wings
    with you can I create dreams coming true
Your thought makes words dull in contrast,

      because

You *are* a radiant sun shining on an unworthy shore.

Poem No. 4 [iii]

damn you,
you press yourself
against my mind
unquenchably eternal.

damn every
essence of your thought –
please leave me alone
I can't use you in a world like this.

torment me not
I pray for your mercy
oh hateful Tyre, you
abandon me for those who can use you.

damn you
oh, beauty of flesh
what can I do with you
and what can you do for me?

Poem No. 5

When eyes sing
 the Earth trembles
 with humility.

The color's not the thing
 blue or brown they resemble,
 green or gray with clear validity

It's not the color, but what lives behind them;
 you can call it the spark,
 or the mirror of the spirit,
 whatever word you stick to them,
 whether seen or not,
 they are Beauty.

 For

When eyes sing
 the Earth trembles
 with humility.

Beauty lives behind eyes
 that sing unknowingly
 of their soul's living condition.

Look, for eyes that sing
    and watch the Earth tremble.

Poem No. 6

A smile or a glance I do not need –
if you smile at another, or glance longingly
then happy I am to simply see
those who make you happy, though other than me.

You caught my mind with a kindly deed
with eyes, with looks so sweet and given gracefully –
Oh, grateful I the day would be
when a smile or a longing look came by me.

Until the day that will never be –
a smile or a glance I do not need
if you glance or smile at others longingly
then happy am I to simply see.

Poem No. 7

Prelude:

God, how beautiful you are,
    Earthly perfections now can I see
And heavenly thoughts aren't even so far
    For I have seen your face and know
        such beauty can truly be.

Poem:

I cannot tell you what you do to me, so let me bore you
    with my attempt.
How grand are my thoughts about you, specters of Beauty,
    real or not,
I have not the blessings to know whether right or wrong
All that I have to conceive is your love sought –
I hope you will never see this pitiful song.
Where to start; an idea I need…
Your eyes are a wonder
All other beauty from them must feed
And puts them under;
They're so clear, I can see your soul, and perhaps
I can find mine there too.
You effortlessly give looks of sincere kindness without
    hesitance
All the world, the new, the old, and eternal, are in your
    eyes of two
What unthinkable grace and unsolemn presence
Your eyes live in an environment of you
They reflect how kind you really are,
A spirit known to few, but blessed your friends are.

I wish I could find the way to show you my love,
Though as worthless as it is,
I hope I can find a way to sing of you aloud; painful wish
Still alive though, spurred by your perfect face that is.
I cannot tell you what you do to me,
so excuse my present.

Postlude:

Words do fail me when I think of you,
So what can an idiot but do?

I think of you and heave a sigh,
I think of God and wonder why.

You're so damn beautiful to me,
I want to know how that can be?

Poem No. 8

The darkened word, the troubled thought
    It haunts me now to be sought
Such pain it holds, how desperate am I
    What strange comfort is by its side
The darkened thought, the horrible work
    It visits me now; how sweetly absurd.

    Love is, a pretentious lie
    for fools who like wholesome pies
    and warm gentle sighs
    and life. Obviously not I.
    Oh, I like the pies
    and the warm sighs
    but the other becomes a brazen lie
    for if only I liked the pies
    and the warm sighs
    and the other too, then life would be a prize.
    Oh well, at least I like the pies...

Poem No. 9

Song Lyrics:

My heart wandered around in disarray
Never thought I could find love in any form or way

Sweet ignorant bliss I thought should be mine
Love sought an odd word, how could it be defined?

I saw boys and girls who drifted by
I never noticed as though they were clouds in the sky.

And then there was you.
You made my heart sing out.
You.
You made my world turn about.

How blind I was before
I couldn't see beyond my blue
And now my heart wants to soar
All just because of you.

How sweet our lives shall be
When we can throw out our blue
For God's union to see
When you know that I love you.

Poem No. 10

Prelude:

There's a flower that I can faintly see,
its existence is a wonder to me
that such a thing unearthly can be.

Poem:

Wonderment!
is the only word I can choose
for a frame of mind
in which to place
your thought.

Wonderment!
at every notion of you;
at the mention of you
my heart goes limp
for sure.

Wonderment!
is the only thing I know
when you are by me;
all I'd need is the Earth
to know you're there.

Postlude:

There's a flower that I can faintly see,
if I close my eyes then it's clear to me
that it's plainly not to be.

Poem No. 11

To forget of you
    will be my hell.

When I can't recall
    what you mean to me

To be deprived
    of your memory

Not to remember
    that once I knew

what the sublime was
    just to think of you.

To forget of you
    will be my hell

for that I can say
    without you, it will be the same.

Poem No. 12

Love, the word is a grotesque thing
    to try and write of you.
And what goodness could it bring
    not to have the sight of you.

So, let me put down my pen
    and stop all this foolishness.
But I don't want this to end
    and I can't you dismiss.

Love, the word is like a vapor
    gone before I knew what it meant
and I can't make love to this paper,
    so with your thought I'll be content.

Poem No. 13

How can I say goodbye
before I've even said hello;
if only it were a simple 'Hi,'
or a friendly 'Yo.'

But I want more than a friend.
From you I want your love;
how you my mind could mend
like only a gift from above.

I can't say 'How are you?'
It's not as simple as that
for I'd mean 'I love you,'
and what good is that.

Poem No. 14

All the flowers of spring
are a loathsome thing
for now and all the while
next to your smile

A sweet and gently fading line
that pronounces itself sublime;
a gentle, subtle hint of lust
filled with no questions, only trust

Through innocence given, received obscene
how can nature be seen, nothing redeemed
so I'm left with the question to ask
how can your smile embrace, or reject its task

The flowers of spring are denied
what your smile calmly cries
they also lack the uneasy rejection
of human confusement as to the question.

Poem No. 15

To dream of you in the sometimes hour
  is to let a piece of me live.
The thought of you has such power,
  you cannot know what you can give.

Poem No. 16

Prelude:

If a line can speak,
what a thought can't know
If a smile can say,
what the heart's afraid
If a sigh can scream,
what a mind only doubts
then, it's in love.

Poem:
Like a picture in a frame holistically
A simple thought I have

to gently caress a thought filled with you
to long for a warm embrace.

Beauty lies in its simplicity
This is the thought I have.

Postlude:

    If a line can speak
what I can barely feel
    in the physical world that's weak
but know in terms that can't be real
    I offer you, however meek.

Poem No. 17

Prelude:

Stay away
so I can't think of you
so I can't remember your face
your subtle face
stay away
I don't want you in my space
with your perfect grace
Stay away

Poem:

Your manner to say
is grace perfected
a passion by day
of night daydream-reflected

You haunt me still the same
you and your sublime face
and yet who can I blame
to see such godly grace

Postlude:

It's painful, to see
how grand you are
and not let you know

Poem No. 18

Poem:

In wonderment I sit and ponder your face,
At how God in subtle ways, shows himself;
In amazement I think undiluted wealth,
For repose, how sullen, you could replace.
Peaceful work, of divine, and perfect taste –
Good God, a maze of beauty's expression felt,
A wonderment of hope to make men melt –
In this frame of words I set your face.
Damn the pompous fools who can't see
The greatness before their eyes,
The sublime is not to them lent,
And fulfillment can't ever be;
If they can't see the joy in your eyes
They'll never know what was sent.

Postlude:

In stoic art I strive –
    I lack the pluck for the heroic
    in creating blaring lies.

In stoic art I strive –
    I lack the skill of the romantic
    and can't read my own sighs.

Poem No. 19

In breathless hesitation I say
    your name
and I wonder if life could ever
    mean the same.

Poem No. 20

Poem:

Your name is the sweetest
    word I've ever known.
Speak it to me now or ever,
    and back to a trembling mess I turn.

Your face – kinder than the one of hope –
    drives me mad with desire.
To think of it still,
    makes Beauty seem a liar.

Postlude:

My words molest you
their impurity of despair insults you
    But, all I long to do is touch you –
    not with hands, but with
    the meaning of their soul.

Poem No. 21

Thus I've found you not to me
    simply because it's not to be

For you are perfection in Death's eternal grip
    and I am human, a sin to fall from life's slip.

Poem No. 22

Words to tears that I never
    said to you.
Love song of one I never told

I loved you as the valley loves
    the rising sun.
The thought of you made my day begin

Poem No. 23

Yellow turns the page,
pale grows the ink
I wrote in love ago.

Fading is the stage,
with you as a link
to the place I used to know.

But think I of you,
of wonders past,
draw the curtain back.

Where on paper new,
my love re-laps
black ink for you.

Finis

What can I say in written lines,
That could do any justice to your character and mind,
And have it come out one tenth as you are sublime?

    I want to praise you, that I do,
    I want to love you, that I do too,
    But what good is that, if I can't even tell you?

What happens when you are in my thought?
The world stands still, and peace is brought,
But there's so much else there too, without a doubt.

    I love to see the sight of you,
    I love to think and write of you,
    But what good is that if I can't ever tell you?

How can I say what my heart can't tell me?
And so I close my song to you, by me.
I hope you find what I only dream of for me.

A final Ross poem appears in a short story of mine. In Six Hours *is about two guys falling for each other over an intense evening at the club and a long night spent out of doors. One of these young men shares personal information about the first boy he fell in love with.*

The following excerpt contains the entire scene where Ross is discussed. In Six Hours *is the penultimate tale in a work entitled* Becoming Real: One Coming Out in Seven Short Stories.

Not many cemeteries are located on the top of a hill, but Josh knew of one. The ancient cut of the river gouged out the soft sandstone into tremendous bluffs that once served as the riverbanks carrying the melted Ice Age to the sea. At certain vantages, vistas cleared of trees opened up and looked down on the endless lights of city and suburbs. On nights like this with a new moon, the sky, and the dark landscape below the level of the ground, competed for the fairest show of sparkle and wonder. Josh's car was like a brooding lifeboat all alone on the South Pacific; the sky reflecting the water, the water the sky, and in the mode of conveyance the lowly survivors watched helplessly, and were not quite sure which way was truly up – the abyss above, or the one below.

Billy and Josh lay on top of a mover's blanket spread over the hood and windshield of Josh's car. Joshua had known about this quietly spectacular spot in the County since his high school friend had showed it to him a few years ago. The car was parked at the edge of the old iron gate protecting the blessèd precinct, and by getting on the hood, they could see over all the tombstones, which with the light coming from behind, looked like murky voids. The city lights stretched to the horizon away from their wheeled lifeboat on three open sides. This late in the night, the Milky Way arced rakishly across the western end of the sky and slowly threatened to retreat, lest the sun get a chance to melt it off from the east. The air was warm, and a gentle stillness pervaded where insect song had recently ripped it into incessant rhythm. Now, only the soft conversation of the young men lilted over the nightscape.

They lay side by side, like twins; legs outstretched and crossed with heel over ankle, arms raised, and bent elbows locking hands behind respective heads. There was a good 'Sunday school' distance between them, but as the conversation warmed, there was a steady inching together, barely perceivable, but committed to by both. In slow degrees they wanted to test if the intimacy they had so easily assumed in the second-floor darts room would bear the fresh air of the open and exposed real world.

Josh started to hum a tune. He didn't pay it any attention. "It must have been great to live in San Francisco. It seems so great there."

Billy thought about it a second. "Some of it's great, but it's not what it's supposed to be. The Gay neighborhood, the Castro, is just a few blocks, and most of the shops are alike, offering cheap crap – rainbow key chains, greeting cards with pictures of drag queens, and window after window of clothes that look all alike. I missed home, where the people are real, and the Gays diverse. I mean, look at us tonight – Jason and Sam, and you and me, we all looked totally different, we don't match; we don't pretend to be anything other than what we appear. In my opinion, I'm glad we're here. It's our job to make this place better by staying, and not ghettoizing ourselves by the Bay." Billy thought he'd gotten too heated, so he looked for a conventional comment to restore balance. "But hey, this spot is great. It's really beautiful here."

"Yeah. I like to come here when I have to think about stuff. And once, I brought my friend from school here, Meg. Tonight reminds me of that." A few notes leaked out of the tune bouncing in his head. "It was after she and her sister, and my friend Helen, went to see the *Rocky Horror Picture Show*. Weird thing is, she knew about me being Gay even then. While Helen and May were getting the tickets, Meg and I stayed in line, and she told me: 'You should go out with me and my Gay friends some night.' I couldn't say anything – I wasn't ready, and she saw that." Josh lowered the arm closest to Billy's side. He scooted imperceptibly towards him. "Before the movie started, a preview for *My Beautiful Laundrette* played. Two guys kiss in it, and the theater erupted in a mixture of cheers and catcalls, and I thought to myself – 'Is that who I am?' I never saw two guys kissing before that, can you believe it? It was like seeing a sunrise for the first time – I mean, yeah, I saw guys fake kiss on *SNL* and shows like that, but on that big screen, it was clear as day, these guys were kissing like they meant it; like the whole world depended on it." Josh's hand reached out and struck Billy's thigh in good humor. He laughed self-consciously. "I know that makes no sense."

Billy struck Josh's thigh in return. "It makes sense. I know." Internally Billy was swallowing down his discomfort, because he did know, and maybe many others would not understand Josh as he did. "So, your friend, Meg, is 'sensitive?'"

"Yes, in fact she told me after we left this cemetery that this place made her uncomfortable. Too much energy; too many emotions she said. I guess I owe my life to her, 'cause she helped me come to a crisis recently – helped me come out."

"How?" Billy's hand came down and lingered on Josh's leg. He moved closer.

"I don't think she indented it, because she had a lot on her plate to deal with, but she gave me a Tarot card reading. At first those in the room who know about these things said my cards laid out in front of me was 'a love reading.' But in detail, there were many bad things. Meg said I was blocked – hidden. If I solved what was blocking my path forward, then the 'Sun Card' was my future." His hand came down on top of Billy's, and stayed there. "You know what the Sun Card means?"

"No—"

"It means rebirth."

"You're saying you came out because of a Tarot reading?"

"Not exactly – It's just that the cards toppled down on me like the straw breaking the camel's back. It was time, and Meg, wanting to or not, gave me the final push." Josh's mood suddenly darkened. He propped himself up on an elbow and rolled to face Billy. "You ever had a girlfriend?"

He sounded incredulous. "Me? No—"

"Good. It ain't right. In high school I had one. I guess she got smart and dumped me. It hurt at the time. Then in my first year of college, I dated this sweet girl who looked like she was really into me, at a time I was not into myself at all." Josh sighed, he cast his look down and played with the nap of Billy's sweater. "I can't tell you, but"—he had to choke something in his throat —"the way she made me feel, broke my heart. I can't... it actually seems like a lifetime ago – I was so stupid, but I thought about sticking with it. Marry her, give her a house and kids and what I thought she needed for a 'happy life,' and not be 'gay.' Stupid, stupid – then I had to do the right thing, which I know she didn't understand, and break it off. I really hurt her, and she deserved so much better; she deserved love, just like the rest of us."

Billy picked up the fingers frantically de-pilling on his chest. He held them in forced stillness a moment; forced Josh to hold his gaze.

Josh managed to say, "I felt so artificial – that whatever thing beat in my chest, it was made of plastic, and I wasn't a real person at all; was never going to be real."

"But you didn't come out, then, first year of college?"

"No – there was no end to my dumb ways, because – from the moment I saw Tina's crushed face, I vowed to never deceive anyone but myself ever again. I saw my life spread out before my cold lifeless eyes – a life without love. A life unlived with anyone. That was the wicked spell broken by Meg and her cards."

Billy spread his arm flat under Josh's head. He pushed on the boy, forcing him to recline and rest, while he propped himself up, and placed one leg on top of Joshua's. "So, Meg's words about the Sun Card and its significance; your ambivalence about love versus a guarded heart couldn't stay in balance anymore – you came out because you had to be true, to the truth."

Josh never felt he could make himself understood, and here the young man with the serious features looming so near to him, seemed to summarize him perfectly. He blinked several times, raising his hand to touch Billy's temple at the hairline. "You understand." For no apparent reason, the tune reasserted itself from earlier. He heard it in his head and part of him hummed along. He knew what it was now. "You like poetry?"

Billy's eyes grew into slits, the corners of his mouth drawing up into mirthful peevishness. "Nobody ever asks me that – Yeah, I love poetry."

"Do you know what this is from:

> "Oh thou, my lovely boy, who in thy power
> Holds time's fickle glass, and his sickle's hour."

"Shakespeare," Billy said triumphantly. "Imagine all the gallons of ink spilled to reassure straights that a man like that – who dedicated a hundred and fifty-four of the world's most intense love poems to a man, *his* man – wasn't queer after all. No wonder no one wants to be 'gay.' They try to keep from us Gays what it really means, and say it never existed before we became so irrational and try to force our coming out down their throats."

"Shakespeare, just one of many – one of most, really. It's the straight poet that's the true rarity. Do you write?"

"How did you guess?" Billy's hand bent to Josh's brow. He touched him the way he often did his own forehead.

"It seems you would."

"Yes, I write; mainly pieces that some would call poems – Jen did. They can be long, but without plot or such. I write because it's therapy for me; cathartic. Why do you write?"

Josh frowned helplessly. "How did you know I write?"

"Your eyes." And Billy scanned the big baby-blues that grew even bigger under his watching.

Josh laughed, poked Billy, not knowing that the other was dead serious. "I write"—Joshua paused—"because – It's an act of forgetting for me; to write is to deal with it – for me, to write is to live." Josh sighed a tiny breath. He could not recall a time before when he was confident that the person he was speaking to would understand him without doubt or question. His hand went behind the back of Billy's head. He rose up to sit and face him as an equal. "Recite me something you wrote."

"I can't...."

"Bullshit. I'm the one said writing is an act or forgetting; for you, remembering, so recite."

Billy thought a moment, his attention drifting over the twinkling cityscape, then to the crest of the Milky Way piercing the far horizon.

> "In a flash, or a day.
> In a flash, or a lifetime.
> Love must build on a spark –
> One to consume us
> In a sustained fire."

Having finished, Billy grinned. "Now you."

Josh inhaled slowly, letting out: "This is one I wrote for a boy in my college math class:

> "See them there,
> The countless numbers
> An errant code and retelling
> Of figures new and old,
> And you – you pass me a note:
> 'Hi,' it said. 'I'm Ross.'

> And for me there,
> Stymied by numbers
> Counting my heartbeats retelling
> Of hopes new and old,
> And you – you pass me a smile:
> 'Hi,' it said. 'I'm yours.'"

Billy kicked back to lean on his hands, startled. He didn't try to control the intensity of the face he flashed on Josh. "Are you kidding? That was fuckin' fantastic!"

"Really?"

"You know that was good – right?"

Joshua swallowed hard. No, he didn't know; no one had ever heard or read it before. "I'm…I'm glad you like it."

Billy grinned ear-to-ear. "And who, is Ross?"

Josh ventured to lay his palm in Billy's lap. "Ross is a guy I fell in love with"—he was relieved when he felt Billy's fist nestle in his grip"—he was in my class, and the first day, as the piece says, he passed me a note, like we were girls in high school – funny thing though, in that small class, Ross and I were the only guys. We hung out some, and I fell hard. He's got these sad gray eyes, and an easygoing way, always with a ready smile for me; so friendly and warm. And it sickens me to think how I acted – the more I felt for him, the colder I forced myself to act around him. I was paralyzed that this straight guy would accuse me of the obvious – 'You're a Fag!'" Josh was upset and he transferred this to Billy's fingers, which he kept kneading within his own grip. "The poor kid, he probably thinks I can't stand him, the way I treated him."

In Billy's mind, a quiet spark fought for his attention. Josh's insentient motion on his fingers, though mindless on the part of the doer, drove an intensity to the forefront of his brain. With his free hand he touched the spot, there, right between the eyes. He fought to tell himself to dispel the silly notion pressing there for release. Billy lifted Josh's hand between their view. He forced it to be still. "And you think this Ross fellow, is straight?"

Joshua gave a blank look.

"Because he doesn't sound straight to me. In fact, it sounds like this guy was totally crushin' on you!"

The night reclaimed the silence hanging between them, and then it hit Josh like a ton of bricks. All the tension in his face drained, and came out of his arms. He had never even considered the possibility. "Fuck," Joshua mumbled, "I am fuckin' stupid; so stupid." Then he started laughing at himself. "As you can tell, I'm fuckin' messed up. I really messed myself up good staying so pathetic for so long." Then serious again "I've got complex feelings about being Gay. Just recently out, the guys I like have little to offer depth-wise; the older guys are more alike to me, but it's unfair to let them think I have strong attachments to them. My 'type,' like Sam, doesn't seem to like me. There's one guy, Nick, you probably know him, or at least seen him around, he's this super-hot jock type, but he turned out to be even less secure than me, though he's got bravado to spare. No, I've done a lot of growing in a short time – it's the mind – that's where the connection is made; the heart has second vote." In Josh's internal melody line, the tune played and played, he couldn't figure out if this song he knew so well was happy or sad for him, here on this hilltop; here with the boy he felt more than attraction for. "It's just as you said: 'Love must build on a spark.'" Joshua unaccountably raised and kissed the back of Billy's hand, and saw Billy change right before his eyes.

Billy slowly withdrew himself with obvious discomfort. He slid down and off the car, and without a word walked over to the cemetery gate. He lifted his arms and hung onto it. He bent his head down, and thought it might explode. The pressure in the center of his forehead forced him to close his eyes and rock his head in pain. 'Not again,' he thought. 'Not here, not now, I can't go through it again.' He stood, he breathed in deep as if taking in light from the city and stars to clear his head. He looked out to the horizon and felt like it was seeping in closer to him.

Alone with his thoughts, Josh kept beating himself up. 'Stupid, stupid, stupid....'

Billy spoke softly. Joshua had to come stand next to him to hear. "You ever really consider why your psychic friend doesn't like to come here?"

"The graves...?"

"I don't think so." Billy guided Josh's vision out over the spread of urban humanity below them. "Here, so much life, rushing, passing, missing, and sometimes, just sometimes, meeting – it must be unbearable. Like a tidal wave of feelings for her, and if she's anything like me, she's not a good swimmer." Billy blinked sad eyes, lurching for Josh's wrist and drawing him in. "But when it happens, when it floats you, when it lifts you, you have to be honest and admit that you know it's there. You understand me, Joshua? It's like...like now."

Endnotes:

[i] **Caveat Page:** The quote comes from *The Book of Friendship Verse,* Joseph Morris and St. Clair Adams [Editors], New York 1924, "Foreword," page v.

> With the exception of "Overview" and "Finis," all the Ross poems are presented in the order in which they were written.

[ii] **Poem No. 1:** Oensuality is the power of our soul reigning in the bodily senses, through which we have bodily knowledge and feeling of all bodily creatures, whoever and wherever they may be.

[iii] **Poem No. 4:** Tyre is a biblical reference concerning a prosperous ancient city and its tragic losses; see Ezekiel 27.

~

www.ingramcontent.com/pod-product-compliance
Lightning Source LLC
Chambersburg PA
CBHW041029170626
46815CB00001B/22